Rockets

SILLY SAUSAGE

School for Sausage

Micha... & Dee Shulman

A & C Black • London

For Lulu, the real little Sausage

Rockets series:

CROOK CATCHERS - Karen Wallace & Judy Brown

MOTLEY'S CREW - Margaret Ryan & Margaret Chamberlain

MR CROC - Frank Rodgers

MRS MAGIC - Wendy Smith

MY FUNNY FAMILY - Colin West

ROVER - Chris Powling & Scoular Anderson

SILLY SAUSAGE - Michaela Morgan & Dee Shulman

WIZARD'S BOY - Scoular Anderson

First paperback edition 2001
First published 2001 in hardback by
A & C Black (Publishers) Ltd
35 Bedford Row, London WC1R 4JH

Text copyright © 2001 Michaela Morgan
Illustrations copyright © 2001 Dee Shulman

ISBN 0-7136-5474-0

Chapter One

One of the longest, plumpest, naughtiest dogs in all the world is... Sausage.

Sausage likes all sorts of things.
He likes his family.

He *quite* likes the other family pets.

He likes lying around.
And he likes eating... especially
sausages.

Today he has eaten sausages (of course) but he's also eaten:

Jack's shoe...

...Elly's book...

...Gran's hat...

His family are not pleased.
They are not pleased at all.

The cats are snooty, as usual.

Chapter Two

'What are we going to
do about Sausage?'
asked Jack.

'It's time he learned how to be sensible,' said Elly.

Gran had an idea.

'Look!' she said.

'Sausage can go to school! He can learn how to be clever – and good.'

On the sign: DOG CLASSES. Your dog can learn to: * walk to heel * sit

Sausage was worried.
The cats didn't help.
They didn't help one bit.

All that night Sausage worried.
He dreamed about his first day
at school.

16

But the next morning, he got
up, had a small...

...breakfast...

...and bravely set off for his first day at school.

The cats followed behind.
'This will be a good laugh!' they said.

21

Chapter Three

In school, Sausage was surprised.
The teacher didn't shout at him.
She smiled at him.
She patted him.

Most of the other dogs seemed nice too.
One of them was called Lola.
She seemed...

...very nice indeed.

Sausage did very well.

He wanted the teacher to be pleased with him.

He wanted his family to be proud of him.

And he wanted Lola to admire him.

He listened very hard and did his very best.

He could walk this way.

He could walk that way.

He could walk round and round and round.

And he only got a little bit dizzy.

25

He could sit...

...stay...

...run...

...and lie down.

In fact he was very, very good at lying down.

Sausage was a success!

Good dog!

Chapter Four

Sausage was doing so well, the cats didn't like it one bit. They made a plan.

When Jack whistled for Sausage to run...

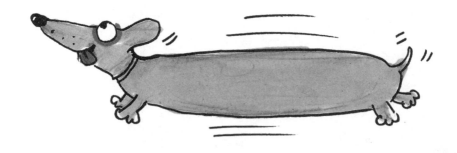

...Fitz clicked.

So Sausage got in a muddle.

When Elly clicked for Sausage to sit...

So Sausage got in a muddle again.

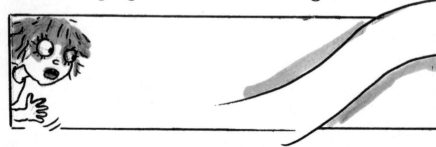

...Spatz whistled.

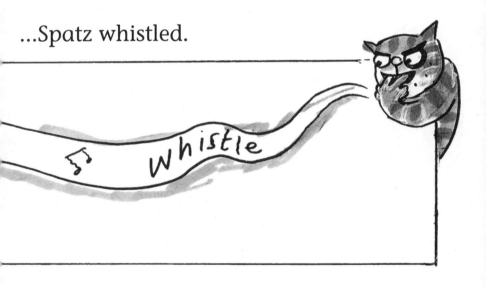

Spatz whistled.

Fitz clicked.

Spatz whistled.
Fitz clicked.

And Sausage got into more and more and more of a muddle.

He got into such a muddle...
...that he made a puddle.

'What can I do?
What can I do?' he worried.

'Don't worry,' said
the teacher.
'It will all be much
better next time...'

Next time!
thought Sausage.

Do I
have to
come
again?!

'And next time,' said the teacher, 'it's the contest and we'll all be able to see just how good you can be!'

Oo-er!

Chapter Five

Soon, too soon, it was the day of the contest. All the dogs were there. All the families were there.

Lola was there and Fitz and Spatz the snooty cats were there too.

The teacher said 'This WILL be fun!
The fastest dog to find its way through the maze will get a prize. Oh, and on the way...

...you will have to...

...get over the fence...

...pop through the tunnel...

...and leap through the paper hoop.'

'May the best dog win.'

'You can do it, Sausage!' Lola whispered.

But Sausage was not so sure.

Sausage stood and worried.

He watched the other dogs have their turn and he worried and worried.

It was just like his bad dream.

The families were watching and cheering.

Come on, Rex!

Go for it Butch!

You can do it, scamp!

Lola was watching.

And the cats were watching and jeering.

'I can't do it, I can't do it,' Sausage worried.

'You can't do it,' the cats agreed.

You're just a Silly Sausage!

No hope! What a dope!

Hopeless! Brainless! Clueless!

'Your turn now, Sausage,' said the teacher.

GO!

Sausage stood and trembled and then...
...he caught a whiff of something...

...whiff of sausages...

He followed the scent trail.
It got stronger and stronger
and stronger.
And Sausage got faster and
faster until he was **ZOOMING**.

Sausage was out of the maze in
no time.

The sizzling sausage smell was so
strong now that Sausage was
almost flying...

...over the fence...

sniff

sniff

...through the tunnel...

...and...

CRASH!

...through the paper hoop.

Sausage felt wonderful.

He ate a sausage or two, and suddenly found he was learning to do all sorts of things.

He learnt to sit.

He learnt to fetch.

He learnt to stay.

He even learnt to juggle.

CLAP CLAP

Gran, Elly and Jack were very proud of
little Sausage.

So was Lola.

And the two snooty cats were...

...very fed up.

Foiled
again!